Getting Away With It

by

Anne Cassidy

First published in 2009 in Great Britain by
Barrington Stoke Ltd
18 Walker Street, Edinburgh, EH3 7LP

www.barringtonstoke.co.uk

ISBN: 978-1-84299-657-7

Printed in Great Britain by Bell & Bain Ltd

A Note from the Author

It interests me how people act after they've done something bad. The right thing to do is face up to it, get it off their chest. Many people can't do that. They try to hide what they have done and this just makes things worse. When Mark tries to cover up the bad thing that he has done, it starts to haunt him. He tries to shrug it off. He thinks that he will forget it. But as time goes by it becomes clear to him that he will never forget what he did that night in Haddon Wood.

Contents

Chapter 1
Back Together Again

Mark missed Katie. Two weeks was a long time to be apart. He saw her at school but she was always with her friends. She was always busy. He thought of giving her a call but he didn't know what to say. His mates told him to forget her.

"It's over!" Tommy said. "Get someone else."

"I saw her out with a bloke," Pete said.

"No, that was her brother, you donkey!" Tommy said, flicking his finger on Pete's head.

"Was it?" Pete said, rubbing his skin, looking upset.

Mark was working on a car when Katie rang him. He spent most of his free time at Eddie's Motor Repairs, his dad's garage. Big Norman was showing him how to check the brakes on a van when he heard his ring tone. When he saw the name *Katie* on his mobile he walked outside to take the call. The cold air hit him. He stamped his feet to keep warm. His breath made little clouds.

"Meet me tonight," he said as soon as she spoke.

"At the sports centre?" she said.

The Sport and Fitness Centre was where they'd met two months before. She'd been playing in the girls' football team and he'd been at the running club. He'd walked past the pitch and seen her blonde ponytail bobbing up and down. It was also the place where she'd dumped him.

"No," he said. "Let's go to Kings."

Kings and Queens was a club they liked. It opened late and the music was good. You had to be over eighteen but Mark and Katie looked older than they were and got in without any questions.

"We'll have to get the last bus back."

"OK!"

"Meet me at nine."

He ended the call.

When Mark got home, Mark's dad was looking at himself in the hall mirror. He was combing his hair so that it covered a bald spot on his head.

"I'm staying at Lisa's tonight," he said.

"Again?" Mark said.

"Is that OK?"

"Sure."

His dad seemed to spend most nights at his girlfriend's house. It meant that Mark spent a lot of time with his grandad. He didn't mind that. He liked the old man. Now and then he wished his dad was there more often. Then they could tell each other jokes and play cards. Sometimes they could have play fights. Like they did when he was younger. Before he met Lisa.

Just after eight o'clock, Mark picked up his keys.

"See you later, Grandad," he shouted, and closed the front door behind him.

He met Katie inside Kings and Queens. He saw her straight away. She was wearing black jeans and a silver top. Her hair was loose, hanging down her back. She looked like a pop star.

"I'm sorry," she said. "I made the *biggest* mistake breaking up with you."

He gave a shrug.

"Did you miss me?"

"I can't hear you!" he said.

The music was loud. Mark felt as if the song was playing inside his head.

"Did you miss me?" she said, in a loud voice.

"Of course I did," he shouted.

"I'll make it up to you," she said.

He liked it when she said that. She was good at making up.

"There's some seats over there," he said. "Let's sit down."

As soon as they sat down, Katie pulled his face round and kissed him hard on the mouth.

"Don't feel like dancing anyway," she whispered.

Mark just nodded. His lips were tingling from the kiss. He pulled her close. Her hair was on his face. He could smell lemon shampoo.

He and Katie were back together. It was perfect.

Chapter 2
Missing the Bus

The last bus drove away.

Mark and Katie stopped running. They'd missed it by seconds. Mark got to the bus stop and gave the post a kick. He was annoyed. He was sure he'd left enough time for them to catch the bus.

"What are we going to do?" Katie said, out of breath.

She pulled her coat tight and folded her arms. She looked cold. Her nose was red. Mark pushed his hands further into his pockets. The snow was falling around them. It dotted Katie's hair and her coat.

"I could ring my brother," she said.

"No way."

Katie's brother, Jon, was eighteen and drove a silver VW Golf. Every time he picked Katie up he asked Mark to look at the paint job or the alloy wheels. Mark knew that he was just showing off. He really wanted to get his own car. Then he could drive Katie around.

"We'll have to do something. I don't want to freeze to death!" Katie said.

Mark looked round. Across from the bus stop was a pub car park. There were three cars parked there.

"Come on," he said, feeling the snow on his face and on the back of his neck. It was five miles to their village and it was bitterly cold. He had to do something.

"Keep watching the pub," he said.

Mark was working on the door handle of a red van. He was using his flick knife and a bank card. He really needed a screwdriver but it wasn't the sort of thing he carried in his pocket. His fingers were stiff with cold.

"Are you sure we should be doing this?" Katie said.

Mark was working as quickly as he could. He knew a lot about cars. He knew about engines and electrics. He knew about brake pads and oil changes. He knew how much cars cost.

He also knew how to steal one.

"We're just borrowing it. Keep watching the pub. Tell me if anyone comes out," he said in a loud whisper.

"I can't feel my fingers, they're so cold!" she said.

A few seconds later there was a click and the handle came towards him. The door opened. He got in and Katie skipped round to the other door. Once inside, Mark put his hands under the steering wheel and felt around. It took a few seconds but with a bit of tugging he got the right wires. He put them together and pushed his foot on the accelerator and the car sprang into life.

"This seat belt's stuck," Katie said. "It won't pull out."

"Let me help."

"Quick, someone's just come out of the pub!" said Katie in a panic.

Mark turned to see. A man was half walking, half running towards the van. He was shouting at them.

"Let's go," said Mark.

The car jumped forward and Mark steered it out of the pub car park and onto the road.

He put his foot down hard on the accelerator and soon they were speeding along, leaving the pub behind. He began to breathe more easily. He'd done it. It had been simple. Quick as a flash. He'd really nicked a car.

Out of town the roads turned into narrow lanes. The snow was heavier now, coming down like a curtain. At least the wind-screen wipers were working.

Katie had opened the glove box and was looking inside, moving things around. She was nosy. She was always doing it in her brother's car. "Do you know the way?" she said, shutting the glove box with a bang.

"'Course," he said.

In the daylight he did know the way, but everything looked different in the dark. Even the road signs had a covering of snow. He took a right turn and carried on. He saw a church he knew, and a post office further along. He felt better. He wasn't lost.

He switched the radio on and music blared out.

"I like this song," Katie said.

Mark felt happy suddenly. He was warm and on his way home. He had his girlfriend back at his side. And in just over a month, when he was seventeen, his dad would buy him his own car. What he wanted, more than anything, was a Jeep. His dad knew that.

The wind-screen wipers were going as fast as they could go and still the snow was settling on the glass. Up ahead was a bend in the road. He could see the big black and white arrows. On each side of the lane was a tall hedge. It felt like they were driving along a corridor. He slowed down to take the bend. He looked at Katie. She was moving to the beat of the song. He felt the van turn and held the steering wheel tight. It was sharp, almost like a right angle. He was glad nothing was coming the other way.

Once he'd gone round the bend he put his foot down. In front was a long, straight road. At each side were the trees of Haddon Wood. He felt them whizz past as he went faster. The head-lights lit up the middle of the road and it was as if he was in a bright tunnel. He looked down at the dashboard clock. The time showed 12:14.

Something rushed across the road. A dark shape. It startled him and his foot shot towards the brake. Then it was gone. He slowed a little and carried on. He felt his heart thumping.

"What was that?" Katie said, above the music.

"Just a deer," he said, turning to her.

When he looked back it was there again. In front of the van. A deer. In the middle of the road. Mark froze for a second. He turned the steering wheel but it was too late. He hit it and there was a loud thump. The van shot off the road as he jammed his foot onto the brake. Then it went onto its side and hit a tree. There was a bang like a steel door slamming shut and he felt his neck being yanked back.

Then it went black.

Chapter 3
Panic

When Mark opened his eyes it was quiet. There was no music. There was no sound from the engine. The wind-screen wipers had stopped. There was no noise. Even the snow fell silently.

He sat very still for a few moments. There were no lights. He couldn't see a thing. He couldn't make out the front of the van but steam was rising into the air. Were they close to the tree? He tried to think back to what had happened. They had hit a tree, he was sure.

He felt very cold. The snow was coming in. He could feel it on his hands and on his jacket. He tried to move but it felt as if there was a great weight on his neck and chest. He undid his seat belt and sat forward.

"Katie?"

His voice was squeaky, as if he'd just woken up from a long sleep. He felt to the side. The passenger seat next to him was empty. He rubbed his eyes. Katie must have woken up before him. Maybe she'd got out of the van to make a call.

To ring for help.

No, she shouldn't do that, he thought, reaching for the door handle. That would bring the police. She could ring her brother. He would take them home. The door opened and he got out and took a few shaky steps away from the van. Her brother was a pain in the neck but he was better than the police.

"Katie?" he said, moving away from the van.

It wasn't as dark as he had first thought. He could see the road and the trees. He pulled his coat tight around him. Where was Katie?

"Katie," he called. "Katie."

He could not see her. His eyes looked along one side of the road and then the other. He stopped when he saw the deer lying on its side. He had hit it. Of course he had. He took slow steps towards it.

It was on the grass. It looked as though it was sleeping. It wasn't as big as he'd thought, maybe only a young deer. He felt a stab of sadness. He wished it could struggle to its feet and creep away.

He turned back. From where he was, he couldn't see the van. They must have shot off the road a long way. He walked towards the steam. When he saw the van again, the wind-screen looked odd. It was as if there was a black shadow over the passenger side.

"Katie?" he called.

When he got closer his jaw went stiff and his throat went dry.

It wasn't a shadow. It was a hole in the wind-screen. A big hole. Big enough for a person to smash through.

"Oh, no," he said.

Where was Katie? He moved quickly, into the wood. The trees were close together and it was darker there. Katie's seat-belt hadn't worked! He had been going to help her fix it but the man had come out of the pub and he'd just driven away and forgotten all about it.

He zig-zagged among the bushes and trees.

He found her on the ground about ten metres from the van. She was lying on her side, her head lolling back. His heart lurched when he saw her blonde hair, wet and stringy. How long had she been there?

He knelt down on the hard ground and touched her. She felt cold and wet.

"Katie," he whispered.

There was blood coming from her nose. He stood up and stepped back away from her. How could this have happened? He took his mobile out. He should call an ambulance.

He should.

He knelt down again. She looked cold and still. The blood around her nose had started to dry. He picked up her wrist and felt for a pulse. He'd seen people do it on TV. Her wrist was heavy, a dead weight. He felt with his fingers. First he thought he had found a pulse. Then he worked out that it was his own heart thumping.

It was too late to help her. She must have smashed through the wind-screen when they hit the tree. He felt as if he might cry. He should cry. His throat felt as if it was clamped up.

He stood up and turned towards a tree. He kicked it in frustration.

He should call an ambulance. But then the police would come as well.

He could call 999 and leave before they arrived. But they'd trace the call back to him. What was he to do?

He could make the call on Katie's mobile.

He knelt down and patted Katie's pockets. There was no mobile. He walked back to the car and opened the door. He felt around on the floor, his hands skating across the clumps of glass from the wind-screen. It wasn't there. Where was it?

When he got back to Katie she was in the same position.

He looked around. Had she had it in her hand when they crashed? Was it lying in the wood somewhere, already covered by snow?

What could he do?

He knelt down by Katie and stared at her for a long time. All he wanted was for her to move, to breathe. She didn't. She was like a broken doll.

He looked back at the van one more time. Then he shoved his hands in his pockets as far as they would go and walked off, through the trees, along the side of the road. No car passed him and he started to run.

Chapter 4
Lying to Grandad

It took just over an hour to get home.

Opening his front door, Mark felt the heat of the house. It was 1:56am. The hall light was on and he could hear the TV from the living room. He stood for a moment and listened hard. His grandad was snoring. He must have fallen asleep in front of the TV.

Mark looked in the hall mirror. He was soaked. His hair was flat on his head and his clothes were wet. His face looked puffy.

He'd cried most of the way home.

He felt awful. It was as if he had a great lump of concrete on his chest. A terrible thing had happened. His girlfriend was dead. It hadn't been his fault, though. Had it?

It had been an accident. What good would it have done to stay there? To call the police? He would have ended up in prison. And nothing would have changed.

Katie would still be dead.

He went to wipe his face on his sleeve but then saw that it was soaking wet. He was shivering. He had to get out of his clothes.

He went upstairs and into the bathroom. He stripped everything off and left it in a pile on the floor. He pulled on another pair of jeans and a top and went downstairs again. The living room lights were off and his grandad was asleep on the sofa. On the carpet was his grandad's whisky glass. Mark switched on the table lamp. Then he turned off the TV. The only sound was grandad's snoring.

He picked up the clock above the fireplace and changed the time. Then he shook his grandad awake.

"Grandad," he said.

His grandad opened his eyes and gave a sleepy smile.

"Hello there Marky, my boy."

"You've fallen asleep," Mark said. "And it's only eleven o'clock!"

"Is it?"

"Look at the clock."

He held the clock out for him to see. The old man put his hand up to push it away.

"I haven't got my glasses on," he said.

He spoke with a slur.

Mark helped him up off the sofa and walked behind him up the stairs. When the old man went into his room Mark went back into the bathroom and picked up all his wet clothes. He took them downstairs and put them into the washing machine. Then he changed the clock back to the correct time.

After a few moments he went to bed.

He lay down and turned the light off. He tried to close his eyes but they opened again. The room was pitch black. It was just like it had been after the crash. He felt his throat closing up.

Was Katie still in the wood, lying on the cold ground? Was it still snowing on her? Was it covering her blonde hair?

Or had a passing car noticed the van on its side? Had they called the police?

He wished he could ring someone and ask but he couldn't.

He hadn't been there. He had been at home, in bed, at the time of the crash. His grandad would back him up on that.

Chapter 5
Katie is Missing

Mark woke up from a deep sleep. It felt as though he was down a black hole. He pulled himself up and looked at his bedside clock. It was 5:07am. It was still dark and he could hear a ringing sound. It took a moment to work out what it was. It was the house phone. He jumped up and ran down the stairs to the hallway and picked it up.

"Mark?" said a woman's voice.

"Yes?" he said.

"It's Katie's mum here. I'm worried sick about Katie. No one knows where she is. She said she was staying at Jackie's house last night but Jackie just called to say that Katie didn't come home, that she was out with you."

Mark was silent.

"Where is she, Mark?"

"I don't know. I did see her last night but we had a fight and she dumped me again."

"Oh!"

"Have you tried her other mates?"

"No, I've just got up. I thought she was staying at Jackie's. I wish Jackie hadn't waited all night to tell me. I'll ring around now. You will tell me if she contacts you?"

"'Course I will."

The phone went dead and Mark stood in the hall-way. His feet felt like blocks of ice.

****

Later, in school, he kept his head down. He stayed in the classroom at break and wondered how long it would be before the news of the crash spread.

"What's up?" Tommy said, putting his head round the door.

"All right, mate?" Pete followed in.

Mark gave a shrug.

"Still upset about your ex?" Tommy said.

"Saw her last night," Mark said. "In Kings. We had a fight though and I left early. It's over between me and her."

"Kings?" Pete said. "You didn't say you were going there!"

"You went to Kings without telling us?"

Tommy and Pete went on for a few minutes about Kings. Tommy made circles with his hand as though he was putting discs onto a turn-table. Pete began to dance around. After a few moments Tommy stopped what he was doing and gave Pete a playful slap round the ear.

"Grow up, mate," he said.

Pete rubbed at his head and looked fed up.

"See you later," Tommy said, and went out of the room. Pete followed.

They hadn't even asked him about Katie.

Katie. Her name gave him a sick feeling. He thought of her lying on the ground. There'd been blood around her nose. He closed his eyes. His chest felt tight. His ribs were like fingers squeezing him.

How could it have happened? If only they had caught the last bus.

He heard the classroom door open and looked up. It was his form teacher. She looked serious.

"There you are, Mark. The Head wants to see you."

"What for?"

"I think it's something to do with Katie Blake. Some sort of accident? Your father's with the Head. I think the police are here too!"

Mark stood up. This was it. This was what he'd been waiting for.

Chapter 6
Telling Lies

They all went straight to the police station. Mark sat in the police car and his dad followed in his car. The policeman was silent. Mark tried to talk.

"What sort of accident was it?"

"Is Katie hurt?"

"Is Katie all right?"

The policeman said, "I don't know any of the details, son."

Mark and his dad sat in a small room that had no windows. While they were waiting, Mark told him the same story that he'd told Katie's mum earlier.

"I left her in Kings. I was home by eleven. You ask Grandad."

"It's some mix-up," his dad said, patting his arm. "Just answer their questions. We can be out of here quickly."

His dad looked at his watch. Mark knew how busy his dad was at the garage. Then there was Lisa. She called him about twenty times a day. His dad's mobile would be full of missed calls.

The door opened and two men came in. One of them had bright ginger hair. He was holding a pad in one hand and a pen in the other. The other man was older and he spoke first. Mark sat very still. He was waiting for them to say, *Katie Blake has been killed in a car crash.*

"Thank you for coming to the station," said one of the policemen. "This isn't a formal interview. It's just a chat."

"OK," Mark said.

"There's been an accident. Katherine Blake has been found near the scene of a car crash in Haddon Wood."

Mark tried to look shocked. The name *Katherine* sounded funny. It was as if it wasn't his Katie at all. He closed his eyes. Inside he was starting to feel a bit sick.

"What happened?" he said, leaning forward, slipping his hands between his legs.

The ginger policeman was staring straight at him. He could feel his eyes boring into him.

"The car skidded off the road. Katherine must have been in the passenger seat. It doesn't look as though she was wearing a seat belt."

"Is she ... is she dead?" Mark said.

"Why do you say that?" the ginger policeman said.

"You said she'd had an accident ..." Mark said.

"Plenty of people have accidents and don't die."

"She wasn't wearing a seat belt ..."

"Why didn't you ask what hospital she was in?"

"Wait a minute!" Mark's dad said.

"Hang on, hang on," said the other policeman in a soft voice. "Give the lad a bit of space. He's had a shock. Katherine was his girlfriend. Just give him a minute!"

Mark looked gratefully at him. His dad sat back.

"Mrs Blake says you were with her daughter last night."

"Yes," he said, "we went to Kings. We had a fight. She ... she kept looking at this other lad. I lost my temper and we argued. She dumped me, so I came home."

"You left her there?"

"Yes. About ten. I got the bus and got home about eleven, I think. My grandad will know what time it was."

"Why not your dad?"

Mark's dad spoke. "I was staying at my girlfriend's last night. His grandad – my dad – lives with us. He'll know what time Mark got in."

The ginger policeman was looking annoyed. "You left your girlfriend in the club?"

"We had a row."

"How was she supposed to get home?"

"She told me to get lost! I thought she'd go with that other lad. The one she was looking at."

"You left her alone?"

The ginger policeman spoke loudly. His finger was pointing at Mark's face.

"Don't speak to him like that!" his dad said.

"Calm down, everyone. Detective Brooks gets a bit upset at times," the older policeman said.

Mark sat back. His heart was banging against his chest. He folded his arms as if to slow it down.

"Listen, Mark, I'm going to be straight with you. I don't think you would have left your girlfriend in that club. Here's what I think. Both of you left the club and you stole a van."

Mark shook his head.

"You drove home through the snow and lost control of the van. It crashed and Katherine was thrown through the window."

"Then you ran away," the ginger one said. "You didn't even ring for an ambulance."

"This is crazy," Mark's dad said, standing up.

"I was at home. You ask my grandad. He knows what time I got in. I didn't run away."

"You could have helped her but you ran away."

It wasn't true. This bit wasn't true. He couldn't have helped Katie. He couldn't. She was dead, but how could he explain that to them without letting on that he was there?

"You can stop these questions," his dad said, pulling his mobile out of his pocket. "I'm calling my solicitor."

"There's no need for that. Like I said, this is just an informal chat. We'll check with the lad's grandad. Then, if we need to see you again, we'll call you."

Mark nodded. His mouth was as dry as chalk.

"Next time he'll come with a solicitor," Mark's dad said.

"How is Katie?" Mark said. "What hospital is she in?"

"Katherine Blake died an hour ago," the ginger one said. "She lay all night on the ground. On her own."

"Oh," said Mark.

"If someone had called an ambulance she would have lived. But now she's dead."

"Come on, Mark, let's get out of here," his dad said.

Mark blinked quickly to hold back the tears. He would not cry. Not in front of them. He would not.

Chapter 7
The Funeral

There were two more meetings at the police station. The second one was on the day of Katie's funeral. His dad had been too busy to come, but the solicitor, Mr Day, was there. The ginger policeman, Detective Brooks, was asking the questions.

Mark kept to his story. Mr Day took notes on a pad in front of him. The police had spoken to his grandad and he'd told them that, yes, Mark had been home by eleven o'clock. Mark went over his story again and again.

After about an hour the solicitor stood up.

"We're leaving now," he said. "You can call us if you have any new evidence."

"Don't you worry," Detective Brooks said. "We will."

Mark walked home. It was cold and wet and the rain felt like it might turn to snow again at any moment. He pulled his hood up and walked with his face down. He looked at his watch. It was almost eleven o'clock and the funeral was at one.

His hand was cold. Each drop of rain felt like liquid ice.

How had he got to this? Just a week ago he had been happy. Katie had called him and they'd agreed to meet at Kings. They were going to make up. He was going to have his arms around his girlfriend again. Everything was going to be all right.

Now she was dead.

The police thought he was to blame. In a way, he was. He'd lost control of the car. It had crashed into a tree. Katie had been thrown through the front window and when he'd found her he had been sure she was dead. He'd really, really thought she was dead.

But she'd been alive. She had lain on the ground for five hours.

The police said that a milk van had passed by at six. The driver was high up in his seat so he noticed the van just off the road. He got out and looked around. When he found Katie, he said, she was still breathing. Just. He took his coat off and covered her and rang for an ambulance.

Mark had left her there. He had honestly, honestly thought that she was dead.

He could have saved her.

That was why he felt sick all the time. That was why he kept crying. That was why he lay on his bed most of the day, his legs curled up.

Everyone thought he was upset about his girlfriend's death.

Only he knew the truth.

When he got home he took his wet clothes off. He changed into his dark trousers and shirt. He put his black shoes on. He wanted to look smart for the funeral.

The doorbell rang. He was ready so he went downstairs.

It was Jon Blake, Katie's brother. He was wearing a dark suit. It made his skin look white, like paper. He was holding his car keys, passing them from one hand to another.

"All right, Jon?" Mark said. "Come in. I'm just getting ready for the church."

"No," Jon said.

He stood on the doorstep. Behind him the rain was pouring down. A blast of cold air came into the hall-way.

"What's up?" Mark said.

"We don't want you at the funeral. My mum doesn't want you there."

"Why not?"

"If it weren't for you, Katie would still be alive."

"The police haven't charged me ..." Mark said.

"We don't want you at the funeral," Jon said, stepping backwards, away from the door, along the garden path towards his silver car.

"This isn't right!"

"You think you've got away with it," Jon called. "Well, you haven't."

Mark closed the door. He looked down at his smart trousers and polished shoes. A spark of anger made him clench his fists. He would have done anything to save Katie. If he'd thought for one second that she was alive, he would have rung for an ambulance.

But he couldn't tell that to anyone because he hadn't been there.

The police couldn't prove a thing.

Jon was right. He did think he'd got away with it.

****

That night he couldn't sleep. It was exactly one week since the crash. When he looked at his bedside clock he saw that it was 12:14. The exact time of the crash. He closed his eyes. He was tired but it was hard to slip off into sleep.

Then he had a strange dream.

In his dream he was lying in bed. His mobile gave a low beep. Someone had sent him a message. In his dream he reached across and picked up his phone. He didn't bother to put the bedside light on because the odd thing was that the screen of his phone was lit up. It said *One New Message*.

Drowsy and rubbing his eyes, Mark pressed the button to open up the message. The words gave him a fright.

Help me, Mark. Don't leave me. I love you. K.

In his dream he tossed the phone away and pulled the sheet up so that it covered his head.

Then he woke up. He looked at the clock on his bedside table. It showed the time, 12:14. The exact same time that he'd gone to sleep. Had it stopped? He reached out for his mobile to check the time. But it wasn't where he normally left it. He put his bedside light on.

His mobile was on the carpet near the foot of the bed. As if he'd thrown it there. He picked it up. He was puzzled. He looked at the screen. The time was 12:14. He pressed the button to see his call history. The last call he'd got was from his dad that afternoon.

He let out a sigh of relief. Of course it was. He'd had a bad dream, that was all.

It was the day of Katie's funeral. That was why he was freaked out.

Chapter 8
One New Message

The next week went quickly. Mark went back to school. Some kids were a bit funny with him, but others were all right.

Tommy and Pete were around a lot.

"You had nothing to do with it, mate, we know that!" Tommy said.

"Don't let the police fit you up," Pete said, and did a few air punches as if he was in a fight. "You don't want to spend years in prison for something you haven't done. Although you could escape. You could get your bed sheets and tie them to the bars and climb out."

"Don't be a donkey!" Tommy said, smacking him on the arm.

Mark listened as they argued. After a while it went quiet. Then he looked up and they were gone. He was alone in the classroom. That was how it was all week. He was so wound up in his own thoughts that he didn't notice what was going on around him.

His dad felt sorry for him.

"You're going through a bad time, son. I don't know if it makes you feel any better but it's your birthday in a couple of weeks' time. I'm planning some driving lessons for you. And I'm going to buy you a car. That should cheer you up a bit."

The lads in his dad's garage looked awkward and spoke to him without joking for once.

"Sorry to hear about your news, Mark," Big Norman said.

"Worst thing, someone dying," Eddie said.

Mark nodded and got on with stuff. A lot of the time he spent doing wheel checks and testing the electrical equipment in the garage. He kept busy. Inside he felt numb. As if his feelings had been put on 'pause' like on a DVD. He still cried a bit, but every day he felt himself getting further away from that night. A couple of times he was working, at school or in the garage, or he was chatting to his grandad, and he found he hadn't thought about Katie at all. For an hour or maybe two.

Things got bad again when he went to bed. That was when his guilt seemed to uncurl from inside him. It seemed to chew at his insides. Sometimes he felt he couldn't stand it. He got up and walked round the dark room, his heart thumping.

It hadn't been his fault. He hadn't meant for it to happen.

A week after the funeral he was walking home from school and heard a beeping sound. When he looked round he saw a car had stopped. The door opened and the ginger detective got out.

"All right, Mark?" he said. "Thought any more about that night in Haddon Wood?"

Mark frowned. He felt he should say something, but the policeman got back into his car and drove off without a second look.

That night he tried to stay up as late as he could. His dad was staying at his girlfriend's. It was exactly two weeks since the night of the crash. He kept thinking about the stupid dream he'd had the week before. He watched DVDs one after the other. His grandad came in about eleven.

"I'm off to bed, Marky."

"See you in the morning."

He stayed up. He watched a film he'd seen before and felt his eyelids get heavy. A couple of times they closed and he jerked awake again. He waited until the clock said 1:25. Then he went up to bed.

It was stupid to remember the dream. It was just that, a dream.

He went to bed and soon he was asleep.

Some time later a noise woke him up. A beep.

He lay still. Maybe he was hearing things. The heating sometimes made noises in the night. Then he heard it again. Another beep. He knew that sound. It was a message on his mobile.

He opened his eyes. He looked at the bedside clock. He saw that the time was 12:14. He rubbed his eyes. It couldn't be. That was hours ago. His mobile beeped for a third time.

53

Was he dreaming? He sat up slowly and reached out for his mobile. Before he touched it he could see that the screen was lit up. He picked it up. The words were there.

One New Message.

He thought about putting it down. Leaving it. Not looking at the message. He stopped. His dad was out. It could be from him. It could be important.

He pressed the button and the message came up.

How could you leave me, Mark? How could you? K.

He dropped it onto his bed, as if it was too hot to hold. He pushed it away down to the far end of the bed. He sat with his knees up. He pulled the sheets round him, covering himself, putting space between him and his mobile.

He looked back at the clock. Now the time was different. 2:11.

This was no dream. He was sure of that much.

Chapter 9
Grave-yard

Katie's grave was at the edge of the grave-yard. New graves had recently been dug there. Katie's grave had no head-stone, just a wooden post with her name on it – *Katherine Blake*.

It was covered in flowers. Many of them had died and were dry and crisp. But at the top, near the post were three plants that looked as if they'd just been placed there. Their flowers were yellow and white. Mark wondered how long it would be before the cold killed them off.

It was freezing. The sky was clear and the sun seemed like a tiny, distant point of light. Mark pulled his collar up so that it touched the bottom of his ears.

It was eight o'clock in the morning and there was no one else around. He felt odd standing there. Why had he come? He thought of the night before. The message. He didn't understand it. Was that why he had come? To try and connect somehow with Katie?

He looked down at the earth, the dried flowers, the hard, cold ground. Katie was lying in a box down there. Inside he felt a swirl of emotion. Katie with her funny blonde ponytail. Katie laughing and joking. Katie kissing him until he was dizzy. Now she was completely still. She would never kiss anyone again.

He tried to focus. Was it possible to connect with the dead?

He stood for a few moments but felt nothing. In his head he started to say the word *Sorry*, over and over again.

A powerful scent hit him. It wasn't the flowers. It was the smell of lemons. He closed his eyes. Katie's hair. It got in the way when they were kissing. He was always combing it back with his fingers. When he got close he could smell the shampoo that she used. Lemons.

He turned to go. He walked along the path towards the exit. He felt the cold nipping at his neck and the back of his ears. When he got to the stone arch and the gates, he turned back for the last time. He looked across hundreds of head-stones until he picked out Katie's grave.

There was someone else standing there. A woman. Her head was bent over as if she was praying. That was odd. He hadn't noticed her pass by him. He began to shiver as a sharp wind came from behind him. It bent the branches of the trees and pulled at the long grasses.

The woman's hair was blowing in the breeze. Long yellow hair.

He stood very still. In a second she would turn and look at him.

He didn't want to see her. He *did not* want to see her face. He wanted to move, to walk away. But for some reason he could not.

He closed his eyes tightly. He held his breath. His arms and neck went stiff. He couldn't move. He was like a statue.

When he opened his eyes again there was no one there.

He was alone in the grave-yard.

Chapter 10
New Phone

The new mobile was expensive but his dad didn't mind.

"You deserve a treat, son," he said, giving it to him. "I've set it all up. It's got a new SIM card and a new number. That's what you wanted, wasn't it?"

Mark nodded, taking the slim black phone from his dad. It was perfect.

"I gave your old handset to Eddie."

His dad's girlfriend, Lisa, was in the driving seat of her car. She waved at him and then revved the engine up so that his dad had to look around.

"I'm coming!" he shouted.

"How long will you be away?" Mark said.

"A few days? Till the weekend. One of the lads from the garage will pick my car up in the morning. One of the shock absorbers needs changing. I've left the keys on the hall table."

"Have a good time," said Mark.

"We will," his dad called, going back to Lisa's car. "Remember, only ten days or so until your birthday!"

Mark nodded. He hadn't thought about his birthday for ages. It just wasn't important.

Today it was three weeks since Katie died. He hadn't been allowed to go to the funeral two weeks before. One week before he'd stood in the grave-yard and tried to connect with her. Each week at the exact time of the crash he'd got a phone message from her.

It was mad.

It was crazy.

Anyone in their right mind would just laugh it off.

Tonight he had a different phone. Tonight he would not get a beep and the words *One New Message*. He would not.

Things hadn't been good at school. That week he'd noticed that kids were avoiding him. One day he'd seen Jon Blake's silver VW parked outside the gates and some kids standing round talking to him. Another day he'd seen Detective Brooks sitting in his car near his house.

He spent a lot of time on his own.

At first he hadn't minded. But after a while it got lonely. When he found Tommy and Pete sitting on a bench in the playground he was glad. He went across and sat beside them.

"All right, mates?" he said, in a jolly way.

Tommy nodded. In his hand was his mobile. He was writing a text. He was staring at the screen.

"What you up to?" he said to Pete.

"This and that," Pete said.

"Did you see the match on TV the other night?" Mark said. "That goal in the last minute! That was good."

"I know! It was the best goal all season!"

Pete stood up and began to jump from side to side, his hands up as if he was a goalkeeper. Mark smiled. Tommy stood up, put his mobile phone in his trouser pocket, and gave Pete a push.

"Come on, donkey. We've got to go."

Pete looked confused and followed Tommy across the playground.

Mark was left sitting on his own.

He went to bed before midnight. He turned the lights off and lay in the dark, wide awake. He looked at the clock. 11:58. If he could get through tonight. If he could lie in bed and wait until the clock said 12:14. Then, when no call came, he would know that it was all OK.

School didn't matter. He didn't like it much anyway. He didn't need good exam results. He could leave and go to work in his dad's garage. The guys who worked there liked him.

He looked at the clock. 12:02.

He could become a brilliant mechanic. He could be better than any of them. When people brought their cars in they would say, *I want Mark to service my car!*

The bedside clock showed 12:05.

And in a short while he would be seventeen. He didn't need driving lessons. He could drive already. He would put in for a driving test as soon as he could. He knew the Highway Code off by heart. Within months he would have his full licence. Then he could drive on his own, anywhere he pleased.

He looked at the red numbers glowing in the dark. 12:11.

He would try to forget the events of the last three weeks. What had happened was bad. It was the worst thing that could have happened. Katie was dead. But it hadn't been his fault.

12:13.

He watched the clock, his mouth open, his breath caught in his throat. In a second it would change. In just a second.

A beep sounded. It was long and hard and seemed to stab into his ears. His new phone. The clock said 12:14.

He sat up. He picked up the new mobile. *One New Message.*

I love you. I want to be with you forever. K.

An hour later he was walking up and down in his room. He'd put the light on and the room was bright. He would not sit in the darkness waiting for Katie to contact him.

This couldn't go on. Was it going to happen every Thursday night for the rest of his life? He couldn't let it. It hadn't been his fault. He had to do something. He got dressed. He looked out the window. It was snowing again, just like that night three weeks before.

What if it had been him that had been thrown through the wind-screen? What if he'd been lying on the ground in the wood? He might have died. He tried to picture in his mind what it would have looked like. Him, Mark, hurt and bleeding. Would he have survived the night?

He had to go back to Haddon Wood.

He had to.

He grabbed his coat and went quietly down the stairs. On the hall table were his dad's car keys. He picked them up. When he opened the front door the snow swirled around him. He got in the car and drove off.

Chapter 11
The Longest Night

He drove fast, the head-lights of his dad's car bouncing off the bends and the hedges. The snow was coming towards him like a blizzard. A couple of cars passed the other way. When he got to Haddon Wood he came to a sudden stop across the road from where he'd crashed weeks before. He turned the engine and the lights off. It was completely silent and dark. Pitch black. He got out. He closed the car door quietly and heard the sharp click it made.

Nothing moved in the wood.

He found the exact spot where Katie had been. The ground had a thin layer of snow. Was it as cold as it had been three weeks before, on the night of the crash? He zipped up his jacket. His dad's car had been warm. Now he felt frozen.

He walked up and down.

It would have been better if he had died on that night. If only the van had hit the deer at a different angle. Then it would have spun the other way so that it hit a tree on the driver's side. Katie would still have been hurt but he would have died from the impact. Then people would not blame him for what happened.

He wouldn't blame himself for leaving Katie on her own.

He sat down by the tree. Maybe it wasn't too late. Maybe if he sat there all night long, in the snow, then he would go into a deep, long sleep and not wake up. Then Katie's family would be happy. The kids from school would be happy.

He pulled his knees up and sat there. He looked at his mobile. It was 1:28. He would stay there, in the woods, just as Katie had done. He would sit in the bitter cold until the morning. His dad was out. His grandad was asleep. No one would know that he wasn't home.

He would spend the night in Haddon Wood. It would be as if Katie was there and he was looking after her. He would not leave her on her own again.

Maybe Katie would forgive him.

After a while he thought he heard the sounds of a car passing. Then another. Then it was quiet. He put the hood of his jacket up and lay down, his head on the soft ground underneath the tree. He stared into the darkness.

Later he closed his eyes. He felt his chin trembling and pulled the tie on his hood. His ears felt cold. His toes felt hard. He moved his knees up to his chest. He could feel the snow dotting his face.

Just like Katie.

Then he fell asleep.

A noise woke him. A sudden cry like the screech of brakes. He sat up his back against the tree. He looked around. The wood seemed darker. It was inky black. He stared into the trees and bushes. He had no idea what had made the noise.

The snow stopped. The woods looked deep as though they went on for miles. The snow from the ground had melted and everything was black or grey. The air was still cold though. He could see his breath in clouds. The trees were still. Nothing moved. It was like the grave-yard.

He closed his eyes. He would try to sleep. That way he could get through the night. He looked up at the tree above him. He could just see the lower branches. They had no leaves. They were bare and looked like twisted fingers. Was that what Katie had seen that night? When she looked up from where she was lying?

He felt a stab of sorrow. Poor Katie. How could he have left her like that? Just to save his own skin.

Much later he sat up and hugged himself to keep out the cold. He rocked back and forth. How long would the night go on? How much longer did he have to stay there?

A lifetime?

He slept. He woke. He turned around and faced the tree. The wood was at his back. He didn't care. He slept. He woke. He slept again.

There were odd noises. More cars going along the road through the wood. He opened his eyes. The darkness was different. It was lighter. It was blue and grey. He sat up. He felt stiff. He was cold but he hardly noticed it. It was morning, he was sure. He put his hand in his jacket pocket searching for his phone. His fingers were stiff but he pulled it out. It was 6:09.

It was morning.

He'd spent the night in the woods.

He'd done it.

He drove home slowly, carefully. The lights were off and he went quietly up to his room. He didn't get undressed, he just pulled the bed cover round him. Then he went to sleep again.

****

A week later he sat in his room at midnight. This time he would wait for Katie's message. When the time on the clock read 12:14 he held his breath. He waited for the beep. He waited to hear from Katie again. Her message from the grave.

But no beep came and the time changed to 12:15.

He lay back. There was no message. Maybe it was over. Maybe, after he'd stayed out all night in Haddon Park, Katie had forgiven him.

Chapter 12
Happy Birthday

On his birthday Mark got up early. The radio was playing a song that he liked. He hummed along to it. He could smell breakfast cooking and he felt hungry. He ran downstairs. His grandad was standing by the cooker. On the table was a pile of cards.

"Happy birthday, Marky," his grandad said.

"Where's dad?"

"He's gone to pick something up. I think it might be for you."

Mark smiled to himself. Was it possible that his dad had found him a Jeep? He'd talked about Jeeps for as long as he could remember. He'd shown his dad photos in magazines. He had shown him websites where they were sold. Mark couldn't wait.

He opened his cards. He stood them up on the table like he'd done when he was younger. There were five. He felt a tiny sting when he saw that there was none from his mates.

And of course there was none from Katie.

For a few seconds he tried to think what it would have been like if Katie had not died. She would have sent him several texts by now and there would be a giant card from her, and later in the day a present that was wrapped up in fancy paper.

They would have gone out somewhere special. Maybe there might have been a surprise birthday party. Why not? Pete and

Tommy and a few of his other mates would have organised it.

But none of this would happen now.

He felt angry all of a sudden. Why should he care? He'd suffered as well as Katie. He'd had the guilt and the strange texts and lost all his mates. Then he'd paid the price for it by sitting in the cold wood all night long. He'd been ready to die out there. But he had lived through the night. And since then there had been no text messages at 12:14.

He had to move on. He would spend his time working on the Jeep and pass his driving test. Then, by the summer, he would be able to drive by himself.

He didn't need any of them.

He heard a car pull up outside. He felt his chest flip. It was his dad. He dashed out to the door. He pulled it open.

It was the ginger policeman.

"What do you want?" Mark said.

"That's not a very nice welcome, sir."

"I'm busy," said Mark.

"I just wanted to give you this," he said, handing Mark a card.

Mark looked at it. It had the words, *Detective Robert Brooks* and two telephone numbers.

"The inquest is in a couple of weeks. I just thought you might remember something new. Or there might be something else you wanted to tell me about that night."

"When are you going to give up?" Mark said, his voice sharp.

"You know, Mark, you'll never be able to get past it. The guilt will always be there."

Mark gave a shrug. When was this man going to leave him alone?

"Well, there's my card. In case you change your mind."

The policeman turned and walked away. Mark watched as he got into his car. The man didn't look round as he drove off. Mark shoved the card in his pocket. He went back into the kitchen. The sight of his birthday cards annoyed him. It was as if he was still a child, having them standing up like that. He flattened them all.

He sat down. He didn't really feel like breakfast. The policeman's visit had taken the shine off his day.

Later he heard the front door open and his dad's voice. He went down to meet him.

"Happy birthday, son," he said.

His dad put his hand in one pocket and Mark heard the jangle of keys.

"Got something parked outside for you. Big Norman drove it here. He's just giving it one last polish. Have a look out of the window."

Mark went into the living room and looked out. There, on the drive, behind his dad's BMW and his grandad's Ford, was a grey Jeep. It was old and it looked battered but it was a jeep and now it belonged to him. He grinned at his dad.

"This what you wanted?" his dad said.

He wanted to hug his dad. He wanted to hug his grandad. Instead he just looked at the Jeep, his mouth open in wonder. One of the other lads from the garage was still in the passenger seat, fiddling about in the glove box.

"It's brilliant," he said. "When can I drive it?"

"Now. We'll take it for a spin."

It was like a dream come true. He looked out again. Big Norman was cleaning the wind-screen with a spray. The other lad was still inside.

"Let me get my other trainers on. Then we can go!"

"All right," his dad said, laughing.

He was back downstairs in moments. When they went out of the front door Big Norman turned round and stood back. Inside, in the passengers' seat, the other lad had his head bowed as if he was fixing something.

His dad held out the keys.

"Want to get in, see what it feels like?"

Mark took the keys. The other lad was still in the car.

"What's *he* doing?" he said.

"Who?" his dad said.

"Him," Mark said, pointing to the passenger seat.

"Who?" his dad said, laughing.

"The lad, inside the car."

He looked puzzled. Mark walked around his dad's BMW. He stood beside his grandad's Ford and looked at the Jeep. Was there someone there? There was – he could see the top of his head. What was he doing?

"Come on, son."

His dad walked to the passenger side and pulled the door open. Mark expected the lad to get out so that his dad could get in. But no one moved. His dad looked worried.

"You all right, Mark?"

Mark couldn't move. He was looking at a face through the window of the car. It was blurred. He couldn't quite believe it. He stared at it, his mouth dry.

Katie.

"You all right, mate?" Big Norman said.

It was. It was Katie in the passenger seat. He closed his eyes and when he opened them he looked again. There was nothing there. No one. He gave a shaky smile. What was going on? Was he seeing things?

He walked towards the Jeep, his heart thumping. His dad got in and he sat in the driver's seat.

"Start it up," his dad said.

Mark put the key in the ignition and turned it. He heard the rumble of the engine. He felt for the hand-brake. He looked up at the rear view mirror. He expected to see the road behind the car. But it wasn't that.

Two eyes stared at him. Katie's eyes.

"Oh."

"Ready to go?" his dad said.

"No, I ..."

Mark opened the door and stumbled out of the Jeep. He backed away from it. It couldn't be true. It couldn't. His dad got out.

"What's up, son?"

"You all right, Mark?" Big Norman said.

She was there in the passenger seat, her head bent over. Fiddling around in the glove box.

"I don't feel well."

Mark turned and walked back into the house. He went up to his room and shut the door. He walked up and down. What was he going to do?

What now?

He went back downstairs and into the living room. He looked out of the window. Big Norman had gone. His dad was standing talking to his grandad. He could hear the words, *He's not been the same since his girlfriend died.*

Then he looked at the Jeep. She was still there in the passenger seat. Her head was bent over but it was the same blonde hair. She looked up and her face became blurry.

Katie, in his Jeep.

He suddenly knew, in that instant, at that moment, that she would never go away. She would always be there. In the Jeep beside him.

He felt in his pocket for the keys. He also pulled out the card that said *Detective Robert Brooks.*

Then he made up his mind.

He walked out to the Jeep and got into the driver's seat. He stared straight ahead. His dad got into the passenger side.

"You look a bit pasty, son," his dad said.

"Let's go for a drive," Mark said, his eyes fixed on the Ford parked in front.

"Do you want to head for school? Or town? Or just drive around?" his dad said.

"No, I know exactly where I'm going," he said, putting the Jeep into reverse.

He looked into the rear view mirror and saw Katie's eyes.

Then he drove off.

Barrington Stoke would like to thank all its readers for commenting on the manuscript before publication and in particular:

Lizzie Alder

Larissa Antonio

Vicky Banfield

Kyra Bennett

Linda Brooks

Rosie Dudley

Emily Hawken

Aiden Hooper

Dan Janes

Aaron Kent

Rob Lane

John Melsom

Jade Morcom

Tom Morcomb

Liam Petherick

Jamie Pittard

Sophie Quarterman

Neil Richards

Alex Ruff

Darryl Sedgeman

Sarah Sparks

Chris Brierley Stamp

Richard Stephens

Kayleigh Sussex

Christopher Turner

Become a Consultant!

Would you like to give us feedback on our titles before they are published? Contact us at the email address below – we'd love to hear from you!

info@barringtonstoke.co.uk
www.barringtonstoke.co.uk

Great reads – no problem!

Barrington Stoke books are:

Great stories – from thrillers to comedy to horror, and all by the best writers around!

No hassle – fast reads with no boring bits, and a story that doesn't let go of you till the last page.

Short – the perfect size for a fast, fun read.

We use our own font and paper to make it easier to read our books. And we ask teenagers like you, who want a no-hassle read, to check every book before it's published.

That way, we know for sure that every Barrington Stoke book is a great read for everyone.

Check out www.barringtonstoke.co.uk for more info about Barrington Stoke and our books!

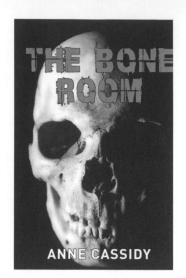

The Bone Room
by Anne Cassidy

Evil from the present, terror from the past ... An empty cottage. A cold room. A thing in the chair. Noises under the floor. Paul and Lulu want to know the truth – but it puts them in danger. Can they stop a terrible crime? And what is the real secret of the Bone Room?

Them and Us
by Bali Rai

David's always the new boy. He and his mum have to keep moving to get away from his dad's beatings. David thinks he can deal with anything. But this time he's the only white boy at his new school. And some people have a problem with that. Can David beat the racist bullies?

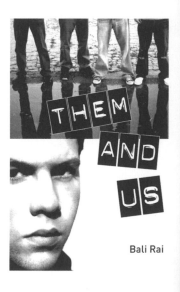

Bali Rai

You can order these books directly from our website at
www.barringtonstoke.co.uk